STAMPEDE
OF THE
SUPERMARKET
SLUGS

STAMPEDE OF THE SUPERMARKET SLUGS

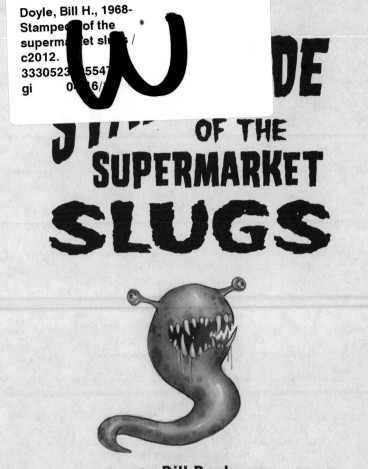

by Bill Doyle
illustrated by Scott Altmann

A STEPPING STONE BOOK™
Random House 🏠 New York

For my big brothers, Tom and John
—B.D.

For Dylan and Addie
—S.A.

Text copyright © 2012 by Bill Doyle
Cover art and interior illustrations copyright © 2012 by Scott Altmann

All rights reserved. Published in the United States by Random House Children's Books, a division of Random House, Inc., New York.

Random House and the colophon are registered trademarks and A Stepping Stone Book and the colophon are trademarks of Random House, Inc.

Visit us on the Web!
SteppingStonesBooks.com
randomhouse.com/kids

Educators and librarians, for a variety of teaching tools, visit us at
randomhouse.com/teachers

Library of Congress Cataloging-in-Publication Data
Doyle, Bill H.
Stampede of the supermarket slugs / by Bill Doyle ; illustrated by Scott Altmann.
p. cm.
"A Stepping Stone Book."
Summary: Cousins Keats and Henry tackle the difficult job of ridding the Purple Rabbit supermarket of a giant Wallenda slug.
ISBN 978-0-375-86934-1 (pbk.) — ISBN 978-0-375-96934-8 (lib. bdg.) —
ISBN 978-0-375-98312-2 (ebook)
[1. Slugs (Mollusks)—Fiction. 2. Cousins—Fiction. 3. Magic—Fiction.]
I. Altmann, Scott, ill. II. Title.
PZ7.D7725 St 2012
[Fic]—dc23 2011012227

Printed in the United States of America

10 9 8 7 6 5 4 3 2

CONTENTS

1

MR. CIGAM SPEAKS

"RUN FASTER!" HENRY shouted to his cousin. "They're catching up!"

"I'm . . . trying . . . ," Keats huffed.

One of his legs was tied to Henry's. They were running on a trail through the woods. Keats heard footsteps right behind them. His heart pounded as he fought to speed up.

Then Henry and Keats burst out of the woods into bright sunshine.

The waiting crowd cheered. The cousins were winning the three-legged race!

Each year, the mayor of Tophat threw a giant summer picnic. Everyone in the small town packed the park for a day of food, music, and games.

"There's the finish line!" Keats panted. He spotted their moms up ahead with other cashiers from the Purple Rabbit Market.

Keats's mom whooped. "Way to go, boys!"

"Watch out behind you!" Aunt Elena warned.

Keats glanced back and his stomach flip-flopped. The eight-year-old Riske twins were right on their heels!

"Don't worry, cuz," Henry said with a wink. "It's in the bag."

Usually Henry and Keats made a good team. They were both nine and best friends.

But Henry was faster and taller than Keats. So running with their legs tied together was tricky.

Still, they just had to hang on a little longer.

"We're going to win!" Keats said with a grin. He was used to finishing books first, not races. Then—

Splat! A sheet of paper flew out of nowhere and covered Keats's face.

"I can't see!" he yelled, and stumbled against Henry.

Keats peeled off the paper. He tried to toss it away. Instead, the paper soared up in the air. Like a dive-bombing bird, it shot down again.

Splat! It covered Henry's eyes. "Ack!" he cried. He made a blind rush for the finish line, jerking Keats sideways.

Keats crashed face-first into the grass. As he fell, he yanked Henry down with him.

The Riske twins whizzed past and won the

race. Crawling, Henry dragged Keats across the line for second place—just in time. They rolled out of the way as the other teams sped to the finish.

Henry laughed. "That was hilarious!" he said, pulling the paper off his face. He shoved it in his pocket so he could untie their legs.

Keats spit out a mouthful of grass. "That was the opposite of hilarious," he groaned. Had he really just wiped out in front of the whole town?

As everyone clapped and hooted, the mayor strode over from the judges' table. He gave the Riskes the first-place trophy. Then he handed a tiny second-place medal to the cousins. Henry pinned it to his shirt and made a funny bow.

"Thank you, you're too kind!" he gushed, kidding around. "Thank you to all our fans!"

"Oh brother," Henry's mom said. She put an arm around Henry's shoulders and ruffled Keats's hair. "Congratulations, Keats. I'm surprised you could even finish the race with a ham for a teammate!"

After the awards were handed out, the crowd broke apart. People wandered over to the barbecues to start grilling lunch.

When they were alone, Henry offered the medal to Keats. But Keats shook his head. He felt lousy about falling down. "Keep it," he said. "You deserve the medal more. I tripped."

"How about we share it?" Henry said. "Besides, tripping wasn't your fault. This crazy sheet of paper was out to get us!" He took the paper from his pocket and started to rip it up.

Meep. A sound came from the paper.

Keats frowned. "What's that noise?" he asked.

Henry shrugged and kept shredding the paper.

Meep! Meep!

"Hold on," Keats said. He took a closer look. Parts of a drawing were on each scrap of paper. A nose covered one piece. An ear was on another. A third piece had an eye—and the eye was winking at him!

All thoughts of the race flew out of Keats's head. "Are you seeing what I'm seeing?" he asked.

Henry's jaw had dropped. He tugged Keats over to a picnic table. They put the paper back together like a puzzle.

Soon a colorful drawing of a face gazed up at them. The face had a patch of hair on top and a pointy beard. It was Mr. Cigam, the magician! He had hired the cousins to do odd jobs around his house earlier that summer.

"Stunner," Henry said. "This must be some kind of magic note!"

Keats nodded. "It was trying to get our attention during the race." He put the last piece—the mouth—in place. Right away, Mr. Cigam started to talk.

Greetings, Henry and Keats!

   I have a new odd job for you. A Wallenda slug has invaded the Purple Rabbit Market! If I cannot get rid of it, the supermarket will be named a hazard zone and shut down.

   Your tasks are to catch that slug and remove it from the supermarket before someone else discovers it. When you complete those two things, I will arrive to pay you for your work.

Sincerely,
Archibald Cigam

P.S. I've left you the recipe for Sleep-Slug Potion in the store's office. The recipe is in the—

Mr. Cigam's voice was cut off. A gust of wind blew the scrap of paper with his mouth off the table.

"Get that mouth!" Keats said. "He was about to say where the recipe is!"

The scrap fluttered in the air like a butterfly. Keats dove for it but missed. Henry chased the mouth as it wafted over a big bowl of cheese puffs. It landed in a jug of pink punch. Henry stuck both hands in the punch.

A little girl licking cheese-puff powder off her fingers watched him splash around. "Yuck," she said, and ran off.

"Sorry!" Henry called after her. He plucked the paper out of the jug and put the mouth back in the picture. But the paper was all soggy. The words came out sounding mushy.

"Theeee . . . recipeee," Mr. Cigam's mouth said, "is . . . in the . . ."

Henry and Keats leaned forward to hear better.

". . . lost Ann fund. . . ."

Then the paper lips became so soggy, no words came out at all.

"The potion recipe is in 'lost Ann's fund'?" Henry said. "Who's Ann?"

Keats shook his head. "I have a bigger question. Do we even want to do this?" he asked. "The last time we worked for Mr. Cigam, we almost got eaten by a crazy shark-headed zombie!"

Henry's face turned serious. "Cuz, we have to do it for our moms," he said.

The cousins looked over at the snack table. Their moms were laughing with the other workers from the Purple Rabbit Market. If the store were shut down, they would all lose their jobs.

Keats sighed. "We don't have a choice," he agreed.

"I'm sure it will be fine," Henry said,

scratching his chin. "After all, how tough can it be to catch one slug?"

Keats's stomach flip-flopped again. When Henry scratched his chin, it was a sure sign that he was lying.

2

THE PURPLE RABBIT

THE COUSINS HOPPED on their bikes and pedaled up and down the hills of Main Street. The library, the basketball court—all of Keats's favorite spots sat empty. It felt like riding through a ghost town.

The supermarket had closed for the picnic, too. The front doors were locked, so Keats and Henry went around to the back of the store, where trucks made deliveries. The big metal door slid open with a loud squeak.

Inside, the Purple Rabbit was quiet and dark. Keats shivered. He'd never been in the store when no one else was around.

Henry flicked on the lights. The ends of thirteen shopping aisles stretched out in front of them. Each had high shelves packed with cans, boxes, bags, and jars.

"How are we going to find a tiny slug in this huge place?" Keats asked.

Henry shrugged. "Mr. Cigam gave us that magic wand after our last job. Maybe we should have brought it along."

"I left the wand at home this morning," Keats said. "I knew you'd use it to win races at the picnic. Or for one of your nutty World's Greatest Plans."

"My World's Greatest Plans are *not* nutty!" Henry protested.

Keats rolled his eyes. "What about your idea to make our own cotton candy from cotton? Or raffle off a playdate with bats? Or when—"

"Okay, okay, I get it." Henry laughed. "I promise no World's Greatest Plans for today, all right?"

Keats groaned. "I've heard that before."

"This time I mean it, I swear." Henry drew an X across his heart with a finger. "Let's just catch the slug and get back to the picnic."

They decided to split up to search the store. Henry headed off to hunt through the meat department, snack aisle, and cleaning products. Meanwhile, Keats checked produce, frozen foods, and the bread aisle. But he found no sign of the slug among the bananas, ice cream, or bagels.

Keats was digging through loaves of bread when he heard a clattering sound. Henry flew

around the corner on the back of a shopping cart.

"Whoa, Thunder!" Henry said. He came to a halt and stepped off the cart.

"Thunder?" Keats asked, trying to hide his smile.

"What?" Henry grinned back. "You call your bike Roget after the thesaurus guy. Why can't I name a shopping cart?"

Keats laughed, and then glanced at his watch. They'd already been in the store for twenty minutes. "If we don't hurry, we'll miss the whole picnic. And the fireworks!" he said. "We need to be smarter about hunting the slug. . . ." He snapped his fingers. "I got it!"

Keats pulled Henry over to one of the checkout lanes. He ducked behind the counter and pushed aside a few grocery bags on the shelf. Behind them, he saw what he was searching for—a stack of coupon books.

"Mom brought one of these home yesterday," Keats said, grabbing a book off the top of the pile. "A map of the store is on the back. We can use it to check—"

"ATTENTION, ALL SLUGS!"

The words made Keats jump. Henry had picked up a microphone for the sound system and was yelling into it. His voice boomed out of speakers around the store.

"Attention, all slugs!" he repeated. "Super

savings specials on slug snacks await you in aisle eight!" He took a breath. "And now I'd like to entertain you with a song—"

Keats lunged for the microphone. He clicked it off before Henry could start singing.

"Henry, this is serious," Keats said. "Our moms will lose their jobs. We need to find that slug before—"

"No problem, cuz," Henry said, gazing over Keats's shoulder. "Done deal."

"Ha," Keats said.

Henry pointed behind Keats. "No, really. Look."

Keats turned around. His jaw dropped. The slug was wriggling down aisle eight toward them . . . as if it had heard Henry.

"Holy moly," Keats said.

In many ways, the slug looked like the ones in his dad's vegetable garden. Its slimy body was shiny yellow with bright orange speckles. Red eyes waved on the ends of two stalks on its head. And as it crawled along, a thick trail of gray slime oozed behind it.

But in one major way, this slug was nothing like other slugs.

"Oh man!" Henry shouted. "That thing is huge!"

The slug was the length of Keats's arm and looked like it weighed at least twenty pounds.

"This can't be real," Keats said. He rubbed his eyes. But the creature was still there.

Keats tucked the store map in his back pocket as the cousins slowly approached the giant slug. Henry crouched down next to it.

"Careful!" Keats warned. "It might be dangerous!"

"Don't be a chicken," Henry said. "It's just a big bug."

"A slug's not really a bug," Keats couldn't resist saying. "It's a gastropod. Kind of a snail without a shell."

"Yeah, yeah," Henry said, not really listening. He grabbed the middle of the slug and picked it up.

The slug's eyes squinted shut. With a *phlurrrrth,* slime squirted out of its skin.

"Yuck!" Henry cried. He dropped the slug. Keats jumped back as its jiggly body bounced

against the floor. The slug's eyestalks waved in opposite directions. Then it turned around and started back down the aisle.

Henry snatched a dish towel from a display rack and wiped the slime off his hands. "Ugh," he said with a wrinkled nose. "I feel like a giant just sneezed on me!"

"We need another way to pick it up," Keats said. He spotted a row of extra-large glass jars on a bottom shelf. He poked airholes in the lid of one with the pen in his jacket pocket. A few steps away, Henry found bright blue oven mitts. He put on two and tossed a pair to Keats. Then they each grabbed two spatulas with long handles.

Following the slime trail, they quickly caught up with the slug. Henry and Keats got on either side. They slid the four spatulas under the slug and lifted. It was like picking up a log of pudding.

"Easy does it," Henry said. Carefully, they popped the slug into the jar. Keats screwed the lid on.

Henry lifted the heavy jar and looked through the glass. "I think I'll name this little guy . . . Squirt."

Keats laughed. "Okay, Squirt it is. Let's take him out of the store. Then we can get back to the picnic!"

As they headed toward the door, Squirt started doing something strange inside the jar. He twisted and stretched his body, pressing it against the glass in different shapes.

"What's Squirt up to?" Henry said.

Keats took the jar to get a better look. "He's making letters with his body!"

Squirt made an *l*. Then an *h*, and more letters. He was spelling something.

lhet me out oar u wil b sory

Stunned, Keats said, "You know what that means?"

"Sure," Henry answered. "Squirt isn't a very good speller."

"No," Keats said. "It means that—"

Just then Squirt squinted his eyes shut again. More slime squirted out of his skin. The jar filled up so fast that slime shot out of the airholes. Glops of it ran down the glass sides. The jar slipped from Keats's hands, dropped to the tiled floor—

And rolled away, taking Squirt with it.

Like a hamster on a wheel, Squirt rolled his jar along the back wall of the store. He had enough speed to push through the swinging doors of the storage area.

By the time Henry and Keats caught up with him, Squirt was bumping the jar against an enormous crate. *Bang! Bang!* The crate was twice as tall as Keats and the side of it read PUFF-TASTIC CHEESE PUFF SNACKS.

"Hey, Squirt!" Henry said. "Knock it off! You're going to give yourself a headache."

Squirt didn't listen. He kept ramming the crate. Just as Keats reached for him, the side of the crate came loose. It fell over with a *whomp,* crashing onto the jar. The glass shattered. Squirt squirmed out from under the heavy wood and broken glass. He was free.

"Rats," Keats groaned. "Now we have to catch him again."

"Uh," Henry said. "I think we've got bigger problems." He backed away from the crate. "Much bigger."

Keats followed his gaze. Henry was staring into the dark crate. At first, all Keats could see were torn cheese-puff wrappers.

Then, looking farther back, he saw what Henry meant. The crate was packed from top to bottom with giant slugs!

3

SUPER SUCKER 8000

AS HENRY AND Keats watched in shock, twelve more Wallenda slugs tumbled out of the box. They piled up in a slimy heap behind Squirt. Like him, these slugs were huge. But their skin was green instead of yellow. And the beady eyes on their eyestalks were black, not red.

"Unfair," Keats whispered. "Mr. Cigam said there was just *one* slug."

"Tell *them* that!" Henry whispered back.

At the sound of their voices, the slugs froze. Then, very slowly, all their eyestalks turned toward Henry and Keats. The black eyes squinted at them angrily.

"Uh-oh," Henry said.

The slugs reared up, revealing their gaping mouths. Even in the dim light, Keats could see something he hadn't noticed before.

"Squirt has fangs!" he shouted. "They all do!"

Keats's shout was like a starting pistol. The slugs oozed forward, heading right for the cousins.

"Ahhh!" Henry and Keats cried at the same time. They stumbled backward through the storeroom doors into the canned-vegetables aisle. Keats skittered into a shelf of baked beans. The cans toppled over as he sprawled onto the floor.

Bang! The storeroom doors flew open and the slugs burst out. Squirt was in the front, leading the pack. Their sharp teeth clicked as their mouths opened and closed. Squirt seemed more confident now that he had backup.

Henry dragged Keats to his feet and pulled him behind a display of stewed tomatoes.

"Why are the slugs so mad at us?" Keats said. He was having a tough time catching his breath.

"Well, we did lock Squirt in a jar," said Henry. Then, scratching his chin, he added, "Don't worry, Keats, we'll be fine. We'll just scare them back into that crate."

Henry grabbed a couple of the jumbo-sized tomato cans. He stepped into the aisle and rolled them at the slugs like he was bowling. Most just jumped over the cans. The others crawled up the shelves to avoid them.

"Don't roll the cans!" Keats said. *"Throw them!"*

The cousins started bombing the slugs with any cans they could get their hands on. Lima beans. Peas. Carrots. Henry scored a few direct hits. But the cans just bounced off the slugs' doughy bodies. They didn't seem to notice.

Several slugs began catching the cans with their mouths. Their teeth tore through the metal. They sucked down what was inside. Then they whipped their heads and flung the slime-covered cans back at the cousins. Half-empty containers whizzed past the stewed-tomato display and clattered around Henry and Keats. Red, green, and yellow vegetable juice sprayed the shelves.

Keats hunched over and started zigzagging down the aisle.

"Where are you going?" Henry asked as he fired off a can of pickled mushrooms.

"To call for help," Keats said. He dodged a missile of beets that crashed to the floor next to him. "This is way beyond what we signed up for!"

Henry jumped out to stop him. "We can't call anyone! If we do, the store will be shut down and our moms will lose their jobs. Don't retreat yet. I have a better idea." He rushed past Keats.

"Wait!" Keats shouted.

"I'll be right back," Henry told him. "Keep them busy." He ran down the aisle and around the corner.

"Keep them busy?" Keats repeated. "With what? A book? A game of chess?"

Keats crawled to the end of the aisle. He ducked behind a stack of pepper grinders with a cardboard cutout of a famous actor wearing a cowboy hat. Behind the cutout was a shelf filled with salt canisters.

Salt! He remembered his dad saying slugs hated salt. Keats opened the spouts of five canisters. Keeping low, he tossed them one by one over the cardboard cutout at the slugs. The open canisters left trails of white as they sailed through the air.

For a moment there was quiet. Then the slugs started making chittering sounds. Had the salt worked? Keats peeked around the cutout. No, the slugs were happily tossing the salt canisters around like beach balls. A few even held canisters in their mouths and poured salt down their throats.

Keats balled his hands into fists. What would it take to stop these super slugs? Even salt didn't work!

"Splurp!" An impatient sound came from Squirt. The other slugs froze. Keats stopped moving, too. Squirt opened his mouth again and said, "Splarb!"

Right away, the frolicking slugs dropped the salt canisters. Their eyestalks went rigid and they lined up in front of Squirt in three rows of four.

"Splarb!" Squirt repeated, and the slugs wriggled forward as a unit. He was like a drill sergeant commanding the troops. Any stray cans of vegetables in their path they either gobbled up or threw at Keats. They fanned out and formed a ring around the display.

"Henry!" Keats shouted. "Help!"

The slugs in the front bit into the pepper grinders, crushing them with their sharp teeth. The rest swarmed over the display and chewed up the life-sized cutout of the actor.

The cowboy hat drifted to the floor. A slug swallowed it whole.

Keats knew he might be next. He couldn't wait anymore. He sprinted and leapt over the slugs, shouting, "Henry! Where are you?"

At his shout, Henry ran out of the housewares section. He wore a bulky red machine on his back like a pack. With both hands, he held a long, wide nozzle.

"What is that thing?" Keats asked.

"The Super Sucker 8000," Henry said proudly. "The supermarket rents out this vacuum cleaner for really nasty messes. It sucks up stuff and seals it inside bags."

Keats eyed the machine. "You're going to use it to capture the slugs!"

Henry tapped his forehead. "You got it, cuz."

With Keats close behind, Henry led the

way back to the slugs. Squirt was guiding them toward the checkout lanes.

"Time to take care of business," Henry said in his best action-hero voice. He reached back and hit the Super Sucker's power switch. Nothing happened. Henry tried the switch again. Still nothing.

By now the slugs had noticed the cousins. Squirt barked out another command and the slugs changed direction.

"Uh, Henry," Keats called out nervously. "They're coming!"

"What's wrong with this thing?" Henry said, shaking the nozzle. "Why won't it work?"

Keats took his eyes off the slugs for a second. He glanced at the vacuum on Henry's back. "You didn't plug it in!" He looked around desperately. *There!* He jammed the vacuum's plug into an electrical outlet in the floor.

Henry flicked the switch. The vacuum roared to life. Now they were ready! But the slugs had changed course again.

Instead of charging the cousins, the slugs attacked the racks of mini snack bags at the ends of each checkout lane. They climbed up past the potato chips and the pretzels and went straight for the cheese puffs at the top. Their weight sent all four racks toppling over.

The slugs swarmed over the snack bags, slashing them open and stuffing the puffs into their mouths. They didn't even seem to notice as Henry and Keats stepped closer.

Henry pointed the nozzle at a slug but he missed. He got a bunch of cheese-puff powder instead. *Thwip!* A pumpkin-sized vacuum bag popped off the back of the machine. It bounced down the aisle.

Keats was really starting to doubt this plan.

"Oops. Let's try that again," Henry said.
This time he sucked up a slug. *Thwop!* The
slug flew up the nozzle and filled one of the

bags. The bag sealed shut and came free from
the vacuum. It fell to the floor with a thud.

"See?" Henry said, grinning. "What did I—"

Pop! The bag exploded as the slug chewed

its way out. It shook off the torn bag like a dog shaking off water. Its black eyes glared at Keats and Henry, and then it jumped in the air. The slug's teeth clamped down onto the fabric of Keats's jacket.

"Hey!" Keats shouted. He pulled away and his jacket sleeve tore off. The slug chewed it to shreds.

All the commotion got Squirt's attention. He took his head out of a bag of snacks. His eyes waved around crossly.

"Splurp!" he shouted through his full mouth of cheese puffs. "Splarb!"

The other slugs stopped eating. One yanked the plug out of the socket and the vacuum died. Two other slugs bit down on the nozzle, crushing the metal.

Henry pulled at the nozzle. But the slugs refused to let go. He had to slide the vacuum

off his back and drop it. The slugs started tearing it apart.

"Okay, Keats," Henry said. "Now you can
say it!"

Keats shouted, "Retreat!"

And the cousins took off running.

4

LOST ANN'S FUND

HENRY AND KEATS scrambled to the small manager's office at the far end of the checkout lanes. They slammed the door shut behind them and, breathing hard, leaned against the metal desk. They could hear the slugs tearing apart the bags of snack food.

"Now what?" Keats said. He eyed the desk phone. "Should we call for help?"

"No way," Henry said, shaking his head.

"I'm not ready to give up. Are you?"

Keats's mind raced. He was freaked out. And honestly he *was* ready to quit. But he didn't want Henry to think he was chicken. "Okay, we won't call anyone yet," he agreed.

Henry said, "Too bad we don't have a World's—"

Keats gave him a sharp look. Henry stopped, remembering his promise not to dream up any World's Greatest Plans. "Too bad we don't have the wand," he said instead. "We could use some magic."

Keats snapped his fingers. "That's it! In his note, Mr. Cigam said he left us the recipe for Sleep-Slug Potion in this office. We can use it to put the slugs to sleep!"

"Good call," said Henry. "We just have to find 'lost Ann's fund,' whatever that is."

The cousins searched the office. They

rummaged through the stacks of papers on the desk. They peeked into the lost-and-found box in the corner. Henry stuck his fingers into the dirt of the wilted potted rubber tree plant near the door. Keats climbed on a chair to check out the top of the file cabinets.

Zilch. No potion recipe.

Keats slumped against the wall.

"You could tell the slugs about gastropods," Henry joked. "That might put them to sleep."

Keats chuckled. He knew Henry was trying to cheer him up.

"Seriously, I don't think the potion recipe is in here," Henry said. "Maybe it got lost and found its way into a bottomless pit or something."

Keats's eyes lit up. "Say that again!"

"Something," Henry repeated.

Keats whacked his shoulder. "No, lost and

found!" he said. "Mr. Cigam's words were all mushed up because of the punch, remember? It sounded like he said 'lost Ann's fund.' But I bet he actually meant 'lost and found'!"

A grin spread across Henry's face. "That's it! Way to go, cuz!"

They both rushed to the cardboard lost-and-found box in the corner. The cousins took out everything. A torn glove. A toy train. One

shoe. Broken eyeglasses. Even a retainer. At the bottom was an old book.

Keats read the title out loud, *"Everything You Ever Wanted to Know About Math and Numbers."*

"Boring," Henry said, already turning away. "Someone probably lost that on purpose."

"Are you kidding me? It sounds great!" Keats reached for it and his fingers slid right over it. He tried again and still couldn't grab the book.

"Whoa," he said. "This book isn't real. It's just a piece of cardboard."

That got Henry's attention. He crouched down next to Keats. Keats slipped one finger under the cardboard. He lifted the fake book and handed it to Henry. Underneath was a small, dusty panel in the floor.

"Stunner," Henry said.

The door was held shut with a wax seal. Big block letters spelled out YLNO CIGAM ROF.

Henry frowned. "What does that mean?" he asked.

Keats read the words again. "I'm not sure. But that's Mr. Cigam's name, right?"

"Yep," Henry said. "And we're working for him. So I vote we see what's inside."

Before Keats could answer, Henry grabbed a letter opener off the desk and pried open the panel. As the wax seal broke, a gust of air shot out. Henry and Keats jerked away as the strange air blew back their hair and swirled around them. It smelled a little like mothballs. Right away, the whole room seemed to change.

Thwup! The rubber tree plant in the corner twisted up toward the ceiling, sprouting purple flowers in the shape of rabbits. The floor lamp danced a jig. And the file cabinet's drawers slammed open and closed.

"Check out the phone, Keats!" Henry whispered. It had sprouted four wheels that spun like a drag car getting ready to race. Then *ping!*, the phone fired off the desk. It hit the floor with so much force that it smashed through the office's thin wall. Dragging the snapped wire, it shot toward the checkout lanes.

Henry and Keats gaped at the phone-shaped hole in the wall.

"Uh, Henry, maybe we shouldn't have opened that panel," Keats said.

Henry shrugged. "Too late now."

They bent back down to look more closely at the floor. Behind the panel was the opening of a tube as wide as a car's exhaust pipe. Under it, a metal plate had the label 1313 HOUDINI WAY—HALLWAY HOUSE.

"Incredible!" Keats said. "That's an old-fashioned pneumatic tube!"

Henry frowned. "Old new-what?"

"Pneumatic tubes were a way to send messages fast," Keats explained. "Air pushes letters from one place to another. This tube says it's connected to Hallway House."

"That's Mr. Cigam's place!" Henry said. "See that? Something's in the tube."

He pulled out a rolled-up sheet of paper tied with a string. He slid the string off and opened it. It was a note in Mr. Cigam's handwriting. Keats leaned closer so they could read it at the same time.

SLEEP-SLUG POTION

Mix one part of each ingredient. Sprinkle potion over the slug.

> Clementine juice
>
> Barbecue sauce
>
> Octopus legs
>
> Nacho cheese dip
>
> Warm milk
>
> Molasses
>
> Best of luck, Henry and Keats!
>
> A. Cigam

"Yes!" Keats tapped the note. "This is what we need! We'll just grab all these ingredients and mix them up—"

"—and *blam!*" Henry said with a grin. "The potion will put the slugs to sleep. They'll be easy to catch. Let's go!"

Knock! Knock!

The sound came from outside the office. Without thinking, Keats asked, "Who's there?"

Henry put a finger to his lips and said, "Shhh." He tiptoed over to the door and peeked down through the small window. "Oh man," he whispered.

Henry waved Keats over so he could see, too. It was Squirt! He knocked his eyestalks against the door again. When he didn't get a response, he sunk his sharp teeth into the lower half of the door. He started tearing at the wood.

"He's going to eat his way inside!" Keats yelled. He didn't bother whispering anymore.

"And he's not alone," Henry said, pointing to the checkout lanes. "Look!"

A few small bags of pretzels and chips hadn't been touched. But every snack pack of cheese puffs on the tipped-over racks had been gobbled up. The herd of slugs was oozing toward the office.

"Hey! There must be twenty slugs now," Keats said, taking a quick count. "How can there be seven more of them?"

Henry didn't have a chance to answer. The office's front wall shook as the slugs swarmed up it, searching for a way in.

Keats started to panic. "This is a super-market *filled* with food! What do they want in here?"

Henry looked at Keats. "You," he said.

"Me?" Keats's eyes nearly popped out of his head.

Henry pointed at Keats's torn jacket. The front was smeared with cheese-puff powder. "I'm guessing cheese puffs are their favorite food. It probably got on you when that slug bit your sleeve."

"Ugh!" Keats cried. He ripped off his jacket and threw it on the ground.

"I've got an idea," Henry said. He picked up the jacket and hurried to the lost-and-found box. Then he rubbed the toy train with cheese-puff powder from Keats's jacket.

"What are you doing?" Keats said.

"See if you can follow my train of thought," Henry said with a wink. "I'm going to send the slugs to the snack-food aisle. It's only one aisle away. Bags and bags of cheese puffs are just waiting for them!"

Henry knelt next to the hole made by the phone. He aimed the train toward the snack aisle and pushed it through. The toy clattered forward a few feet, then crashed to its side in front of the snack aisle. Before the cousins could see anything else—

An eyestalk jammed through the hole. The slug's black eyeball glared at the boys.

Keats jerked back. "The slugs didn't notice the train! They're still breaking in!"

Henry held up a hand. "Wait. Just wait," he said.

They heard a long, wet sniffing sound. And then the eyestalk popped back through the hole. Henry and Keats got down to look. Smelling the air, a curious slug squirmed over to the train and bit down. As it chewed the toy, the slug glanced down the snack aisle . . . and its eyes went wide.

"Yes!" Keats said. He pumped his fist. "It sees the cheese puffs!"

With a "wheee!" of excitement, the slug dove into the aisle and out of sight. At the sound of tearing bags, the other slugs dropped from the office wall with a series of plops and hurried over to the snack aisle. The cousins were alone again.

"There are tons of cheese puffs in that aisle," Henry said. "That should keep the slugs busy for now."

"For now," Keats repeated. But he knew it wouldn't take the slugs long to eat all the cheese puffs. Then they would start looking for something else to munch on.

Like maybe two cousins named Keats and Henry.

5

MIXED-UP MAGIC

AVOIDING THE SLIME streaks on the floor and office door, the cousins crept out into the store. They couldn't see the slugs in the snack aisle. But they could hear them ripping through wrappers and chomping the snacks.

Keats shuddered. "I *really* can't wait to get out of here," he said.

He matched the potion recipe to the map on the coupon book. The ingredients were scattered all over the store. They didn't have time to get everything before the cheese puffs ran out.

Henry tapped his nose, thinking. "We'll have to split up again," he said.

"Oh man . . . ," Keats groaned.

"It's the best way," Henry said. "The sooner we send the slugs to Snoozeville, the quicker we can leave."

"It's not that," Keats said. He turned Henry around to face the pet-food aisle.

Down near the water bowls, six dogs were chasing squeaky cat toys in circles. At least they *looked* like dogs. Their bodies were made of bone-shaped treats. And when they opened their mouths to bark or snap at the toys, kibble fell out.

"Please tell me I'm imagining that," Keats said to Henry.

"Wish I could, cuz," Henry responded.

A clanging came from the next aisle over. Henry and Keats shared a worried look. Together they took a few steps to peek into the cleaning aisle.

A band of ten mops battled a crew of a dozen brooms. Their handles waved through the air like swords as they crashed against each other. *Whack! Whack!* From the shelves, an audience of metal dustpans clapped and clanged. Henry and Keats jumped as a sponge fired from a bucket like a cannonball.

Weird noises—grunts, bells, ripping, and crashing—came from around the store.

"What's going on?" Henry asked just as a breeze blew past them. "And, phew! What's that stink?"

Keats took a whiff. The breeze smelled like mothballs. It reminded him of the air that came out of the tube in the office. Keats nodded slowly as the pieces fell into place. "Remember how Mr. Cigam's house was full of crazy, mixed-up magic?" he asked.

Henry chuckled. "Uh, kind of hard to forget, Keats."

"When we opened the panel, I bet we let in air from Hallway House," Keats said. "Now that air is blowing all around the store. It's making things go berserk!"

"Oh man," Henry said. "Giant slugs *and* weird magic air? Let's get moving before something even creepier shows up."

He handed Keats a plastic shopping bag from a checkout lane and took one for himself. Before they split up, Henry said, "You grab the top two things on the list. I'll get the bottom two. And I'll meet you at the seafood counter for the octopus legs."

The cousins headed off in different directions. Keats moved fast through the store but kept an eye out for danger. A slug and its sharp teeth might be just around the corner.

The barbecue sauce sat on a shelf with the mustard and ketchup at the end of an aisle. He tossed a bottle in his bag and rushed on. A rolling herd of toilet paper nearly tripped him, but he soon made it to the fruits and vegetables. During a quick look around, Keats spotted the almost-empty table of clementines.

"There's only one clementine left, Henry!" Keats yelled, putting the fruit in his bag. "We'll need more than that for the potion. There's a lot of slugs!"

"I've got my own problems here in dairy!" Henry shouted from the back of the store. "Should milk cartons be mooing?"

Keats didn't have time to answer. An

orange ball whizzed toward his head. He ducked and it just missed him. When he looked up, he gasped. The air swirled with bright colors.

"Whoa," Keats said. "They're fruit flies."

Above him, pineapples spun like helicopters. Green melons floated like balloons. Bananas wobbled like boomerangs.

And there! A flock of twenty clementines soared to the ceiling. Then they dipped at the same time in a long, gliding arc. Keats crouched when they zipped past his head and flew back up. As he watched, they repeated this pattern over and over.

He needed to catch a couple of them. But how?

Keats scrambled onto the empty table. Keeping his head tucked down, he opened the shopping bag with both hands. He waved it over his head like a net and waited. *Fft*. The bag jerked in his hands once. *Fft*. And again.

Yes! He had captured two more clementines! Once in his bag, they stopped trying to fly and turned back into normal fruit.

Keats jumped to the floor. "Hey, Henry!" he shouted. "I've got the fruit and the barbecue sauce!"

"And I found the milk and molasses!" Henry yelled. "Meet me at seafood!"

The seafood counter was in the back of the store. The ice-packed case was piled high with raw fish fillets and shellfish. Over the counter, an electronic sign said in neon green letters PLEASE TAKE A NUMBER—NOW SERVING CUSTOMER 56!

Henry and Keats greeted each other with a high five. They went around to the back of the glass case.

"I took a peek at the slugs after getting the molasses," Henry said. He set down his shopping bag and hunted for octopus legs among the heaps of seafood. "Don't panic, but the cheese puffs are almost gone."

Keats felt his stomach flip-flop. "They might come after us next!" he sputtered.

Henry opened the seafood case. "Luckily,

we only have two things left on the slug sleep potion list. Nacho cheese dip . . . and these beautiful babies!" He reached into the case and scooped up three slithery octopus legs. Grinning, he pulled his hand back out. "Now we'll just—"

He didn't finish. Two dozen lobster claws shot out of the seafood case. *Ka-fling! Ka-fling! Ka-fling!* They latched all along Henry's shirt and pants and shoved him back against the concrete wall.

"Keats," he wheezed, the wind knocked out of him. The claws slid him ten feet straight up the wall.

Keats dropped his shopping bag and jumped to grab Henry's foot. He couldn't reach it.

"Help!" Henry shouted, getting his breath back. He struggled, but the claws had him

pinned. "These little guys are really strong—ouch!"

The claws began pulling Henry's arms and legs in different directions. Above his head, the number 56 on the electronic sign turned red. It blinked a warning. Keats stared at it for a second.

"Henry, I know what's wrong!" Keats called out. "You didn't take a number. It wasn't your turn and you took the octopus legs. Drop the legs!"

Henry opened his hand. Two of the octopus legs slithered to the floor.

"All of the legs!" Keats demanded. "You have to drop all of them!"

"I can't," Henry said. He nodded at his right hand. The claws had pinned Henry's hand to the wall. The last octopus leg was stuck behind it.

Keats ran to the dispenser. He pulled out the next ticket, number 56.

"Henry, catch!" He tried to toss the ticket to Henry, but it was too light. It just drifted to the ground.

Keats needed to make it heavier. He reached into the garbage and grabbed a fish head. He popped the ticket into the gaping mouth.

The sign blinked faster and made a beeping sound. The lobster claws holding Henry pulled harder. They quivered like rockets about to take off.

"Hurry!" Henry shouted.

Keats loved basketball but he wasn't always very good at it. This time, though, he had to make the shot. Taking a deep breath, Keats launched the fish head into the air.

Henry leaned forward to catch it the only

way he could—with his mouth. His teeth clamped down on the fish head and the ticket inside.

Right away, the sign stopped beeping and blinking. Henry slid down the wall to the floor. *Click! Click!* The claws unclamped from his clothes.

"Blech," Henry said. He spit out the fish head and wiped the scales off his tongue. But then he grinned. "Nice shot, Keats. Next time we're on the court, I want you on my team."

"Sounds good," Keats said with a smile. He picked up his shopping bag so Henry could drop the octopus legs inside.

"We just need one more thing for the potion," Henry said. "Nacho cheese dip."

Keats nodded and took out the map of the store.

"Uh-oh," Henry said as Keats's face went white. "What is it now?"

"The nacho cheese dip is in the snack aisle," Keats said miserably. "Right next to the cheese puffs . . . and the slugs!"

6

CHECK BACK SOON!

CARRYING THEIR BAGS, the cousins ran along the store's back wall toward the snack aisle.

On the way, an angry snowman made of frozen yogurt hurled ice cubes at them from the freezer section. Boxes of cornflakes exploded on the cereal shelves. Everywhere the smell of mothballs was growing stronger.

"We better hurry," Keats said.

When they reached the end of the snack

aisle, Henry and Keats peeked around the corner.

The slugs swarmed the shelves just a few feet away. Their eyes were closed as they focused on gobbling up the snacks. Only a couple of cheese-puff bags remained.

Keats pulled Henry back out of the snack aisle.

"There are at least thirty slugs now!" he whispered. "Where are they coming from?"

"No idea," Henry said. "But let's mix up the rest of the potion right here. Then we can just toss in the dip when we get it."

The recipe called for warm milk, so Keats put the milk carton under his armpit. Meanwhile, Henry poured the barbecue sauce and molasses into one of the bags. Then he squished up the clementines and octopus legs and threw them in, too. When Keats added the milk, the bag bulged with an orange paste.

"You ready?" Henry asked.

Keats nodded. Carrying the shopping bag, he followed Henry into the aisle. They tiptoed near the slugs. The cousins were careful not to make a sound, then—

SCRUNCH! Keats's foot crinkled on an empty snack wrapper. He winced. And waited for the slugs to attack.

Luckily, the slugs were still too intent on eating to notice.

Henry stepped closer to the shelves of dips. He read the labels in a low voice. "Artichoke dip, chocolate dip, egg cream dip . . . Wait. . . ." He trailed off.

"What is it?" Keats whispered.

Henry pointed at the shelf labeled NACHO CHEESE DIP. On it sat a card with a picture of a grinning purple rabbit. The card said SORRY! WE'RE BUSY RESTOCKING THIS ITEM! PLEASE CHECK BACK SOON!

"Check back soon?" Keats's voice cracked. "We don't have soon! And we can't make the potion without the dip!"

Behind him, with a chorus of burps and lip smacking, the slugs finished off the last bag of cheese puffs.

Their baseball-sized eyes opened slowly. They turned their dark gaze on Henry and Keats. Squirt and the other slugs dropped from the shelves to the floor with a squishy *plop! plop!*

"Run!" Keats yelled.

Too late. Wriggling fast, the slugs surrounded the cousins. Keats and Henry couldn't jump over this many slugs. They were trapped.

Henry kicked the bottom shelf. "Why are

they mad at *us*?" he asked. "It's not our fault the only cheese puffs left in town are at the picnic! We didn't—"

"SPLURP!" Squirt yelled. And then he added, "Splarb!"

Keats shivered. What scary thing was Squirt ordering the slugs to do next?

The thirty slugs lifted their heads. As one, they smelled the air. They made deep loud sniffs, again and again.

"Uh . . . okay, this is weird," Henry said. "Are they going to sneeze us to death?"

Their heads jerked to the side, as if catching a special scent. They smelled the air a few more times. Then the slugs oozed away toward the front of the store.

"What are they doing?" Keats asked.

Keats and Henry followed the slugs and found them banging on the locked front door.

It didn't budge. The slugs turned to the huge window that faced the parking lot. They knocked their eyestalks on the thick glass and pressed their weight up against it.

"Woo-hoo!" Henry jumped around. "The slugs are trying to leave! We're safe!"

Henry put up his hand for a high five. But Keats didn't meet it. Something was wrong. . . .

"Don't worry, Keats," Henry said. "We gave the job our best shot."

"That's not the problem," Keats said. He couldn't quite put his finger on it. . . . It was right in front of his nose. . . .

Then it hit him. "Fingers! Noses!" Keats yelped. "Henry, we have to keep the slugs here!"

"Are you nuts?" Henry said.

"We can't let them leave," Keats insisted. "The slugs are headed to the picnic! Think about it. People at the picnic have been eating

cheese puffs all day. They have cheesy powder all over their fingers and faces."

Now Henry got it. "They'll be in real
trouble if a bunch of hungry giant slugs show
up. We have to stop them!"

The cousins sprang into action.

Keats pointed to the pay phone near the
front doors. "I'll call for help," he said.

"And I'll keep the slugs busy," Henry said.
He jumped on the back of the shopping cart
and wheeled around the slugs. He came just
close enough to get their attention, but he
managed to avoid their snapping jaws.

Henry said, "Get to the phone, Keats!"

Dropping the shopping bag, Keats dashed
around the corner toward the front doors—

And right into a puddle of slug slime. His
feet slipped out from under him.

"Umph!" Keats fell onto his side.

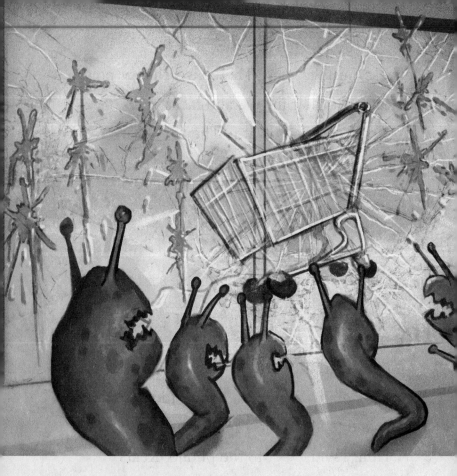

"Keats!" Henry called. "You might want to
hurry!"

Still on the floor, Keats looked back. Several slugs had grabbed the front of Henry's
shopping cart with their teeth. They shook

their heads and Henry was thrown off. He
landed near a pile of shopping bags.

The slugs lifted the shopping cart. Like a
catapult, they flung it at the window. The cart
bounced off, but the glass cracked.

"We're running out of time!" Henry yelled.

Keats got to his feet. The slime puddle sat between him and the phone. He backed up and took a running jump. He almost made it. But not quite. He landed with a splash in the slime. Somehow, though, he stayed on his feet. He stumbled toward the pay phone. He reached for it—

Keats's hand grabbed at air. The receiver was gone. A torn cord dangled from the wall. Maybe the receiver had run off with the office phone. Or maybe the slugs had eaten it. Either way, they needed a new plan.

"Henry!" Keats waded back through slime. "There's no phone!"

The slugs rammed the cart into the window again. This time it smashed through the glass, leaving a giant hole. The slugs chattered happily as they crawled through to the parking lot.

Stunned, Keats and Henry watched as Squirt sniffed the air once more. Then he shouted a command, "Splurp!" He and the other slugs lowered their eyestalks against their heads. They tucked their bodies into balls.

"Splarb!" Squirt yelled.

The slugs rolled out of the parking lot and down Main Street. They were moving downhill, heading straight for the park. Even if Henry and Keats ran to get their bikes, they wouldn't be able to catch up. Or warn the people at the picnic.

The cousins looked at each other, wide-eyed.

"This definitely isn't good," Henry said.

7

STAMPEDE!

"WHAT CAN WE do?" Keats said. "Everyone in the park is in danger!"

Henry searched the tattered snack bags on the floor. "If we had more cheese puffs, maybe we could distract the slugs."

"*If,*" Keats repeated. "The cheese puffs are all gone!" To make the point, he waved around an empty wrapper. Then he stopped. The orange wrapper reminded him of something.

"Too bad we can't make more puffs, right?" Henry said.

"Maybe we can!" Keats said. He ran to where he'd dropped the shopping bag. He held the top closed and shook it to mix up the ingredients again.

Henry watched, frowning. "Uh, Keats," he said, "the potion won't work without the dip. Plus that stuff stinks!"

Keats ignored him. He scooped both hands into the orange slop. It slid through his fingers like a mix of rotten bananas and old tuna fish. He gritted his teeth—and smeared it all over his arms.

"Keats!" Henry shouted. "Stop!"

Keats still didn't listen. He wiped the sticky paste over his clothes, on his face, and in his hair.

"Follow me," Keats said when he was done. Leaving orange footprints, he climbed out the broken window to the parking lot. He rushed to the shopping cart thrown by the slugs. He turned it upright.

Henry stormed over to him. "What are you doing with Thunder?" he demanded. "Why'd you put that junk all over yourself? Answer me!"

"You said we needed cheese puffs to distract the slugs," Keats explained as he climbed into the shopping cart. "Well, you're looking at one." He pointed at himself. "I'm disguised as a giant cheese puff. Give me a push and hop on the back. We'll catch up and lead the slugs away from the picnic. Let's go!"

Henry shook his head. "This is a bad idea." For once, Keats would have loved to see his cousin scratching his chin. But Henry was telling the truth.

"It's the only way!" Keats said. "Hurry! Before the slugs get too far!"

Henry looked down the street and came to a decision. "Oh man," he finally said. "I can't believe we're doing this."

Shaking his head, he pushed the cart with Keats crouched inside. They peeled out of the parking lot and hit Main Street. When they

started speeding downhill, Henry jumped on the back.

"I hope this—" Henry began to say. But his foot slipped on a patch of slug slime. Then he was gone.

Henry fell off and hit the road hard. *Wham!* He reached for the cart. Too late. Thunder whizzed down Main Street. Keats was alone now. And going faster.

"I can't stop!" Keats shouted over his shoulder to Henry.

Henry got to his feet. "I'll get my bike and catch up!" he called. "Hold on!"

While Henry ran back toward the store, Keats turned to face forward. The stores on either side zipped by in a blur. The wind whipped past as he hurtled down the hill. The cart's wheels rattled like they might fall off.

He bumped over a small rise. And there

up ahead, barely visible between two hills, were the slugs!

They'd stopped to chew on a few orange construction cones. Their eyestalks followed him like periscopes as he rocketed past.

Keats shot up over the next hill. The shopping cart caught air for a second, and the front wheels came down crooked. The cart jerked up onto the sidewalk. It flipped over, tossing Keats onto the grass between the street and the sidewalk. He tumbled across the pavement.

"Ugh," Keats moaned as he came to rest in the middle of Main Street.

He lay there for a second, checking for broken bones. But nothing hurt too badly. He lifted his head and looked around. The town was quiet. No cars. No people. No slugs.

Then he felt a rumbling coming through

the ground. Keats jumped to his feet.

Thirty slugs charged over the top of the hill. Stretched in a line across the street and oozing slime everywhere, the stampede of slugs headed straight for him!

Keats's stomach flip-flopped. His legs wanted to run, but he forced himself to stand perfectly still.

"Act like a cheese puff," he told himself over and over. "Act like a cheese puff."

The slugs showed no sign of slowing down. Would they just steamroll over him?

When they were about fifty yards away, Squirt's head turned toward Keats and he did a double take. He shouted, "Splurp? Splarb?" The entire line of slugs slowed. A couple tilted their heads at Keats, their eyes going wide. They all stared, almost like they couldn't believe what they were seeing.

It was a super slug's dream come true— a giant cheese puff!

The slugs started moving again, faster than before. Feeling like a cowboy in a Western, Keats stood his ground. He had to keep them from going to the picnic.

"Come and get me," he whispered.

Keats let them get close. He could see the whites of their eyes. They were only forty feet away. Thirty. Twenty. Keats waited just one more second—

And then he ran.

8

SLUG SHOWDOWN

FOR THE SECOND time that day, Keats was in a race. But this time he couldn't trip.

He sprinted down the street past the beauty parlor and the post office. He could hear the slugs oozing along behind him. The thought of a cheese-puff dinner seemed to give them extra speed.

Keats wanted to shout for help. But no one was around to hear him. And if he did, the slugs might decide he wasn't actually a cheese puff. Then they'd head off toward the picnic again.

Besides, Keats figured he could keep them running around the small town until Henry arrived. He'd lived here his whole life. He knew every nook and corner. And though the slugs were fast, he was faster.

Still, with thirty giant slugs chasing him, he got distracted. Keats ran by the library and down the street toward the diner. Without thinking, he took a quick left.

And just like that, Keats found himself in the town's one and only dead end. He was in the alley between the diner and the movie theater . . . and the alley ended in a brick wall.

Uh-oh.

Keats spun around. The slugs were close. With no time to backtrack, he ran up to the brick wall. Was there a door? No luck.

Keats gasped. Now he knew why they called it a dead end.

Squirt and the rest of the slugs flooded into the alley, filling it with their slimy bodies. They chittered away, excited to have trapped the world's largest cheese puff. Their mouths opened.

"Wait!" Keats held up his hands.

At the sound of his voice, Squirt cocked his

head again. Keats could imagine him thinking, *Weird, I've never heard a cheese puff talk before.*

"Splurp?" Squirt said. He sounded unsure.

One of the slugs inched forward. It gave Keats a quick lick and then jerked back as if to say, *Blech!*

Keats knew he must taste awful. Barbecue sauce mixed with octopus legs and clementine juice couldn't be tasty. The slug took another lick. Again, it jerked back with a *blech!*

Squirt's eyes opened wider. He knew he had been tricked. This wasn't a giant cheese puff!

"Splurp!" Squirt commanded. His voice sounded as furious as a slug's can sound. "Splarb!"

The slugs crawled forward. Their mouths gaped, showing crooked rows of pointy teeth.

"I'm not a cheese puff!" Keats shouted.

Squirt didn't seem to care anymore if Keats was a cheese puff or not. The slugs were so close now, he could smell the cheese on their cold breath.

Keats pressed his back against the brick wall. The slugs inched even nearer, getting ready to bite down—

"Hold it right there, Squirt!" Henry screeched into the alley on his bike. He had an orange vacuum-bag ball under one arm.

The slugs paused. They twisted around to look at him.

"Henry!" Keats shouted. "Holy moly, am I glad to see you!"

The slugs eyed Henry for a moment. Squirt gave a slug shrug, and they all turned back to Keats. He shuddered as their eyes fixed on him again.

"I know I said to knock off the World's Greatest Plans," Keats called to Henry. "But if you have one, I promise to never make fun of them again!"

Henry smiled. "I thought you'd never ask." He unpinned the second-place medal from his shirt. "My World's Greatest Plan is to share this medal."

Henry threw it like a disk. It spun through the air toward Keats, who reached up and caught it. But what was he supposed to do with it?

"Don't worry, cuz," Henry said with a wink, just like he had during the race. "It's in the *bag*."

Aha! Keats returned the wink. He unhooked the pin from the medal and held it out like a little sword.

Squirt's lips seemed to form a smile at the

silly weapon. And Keats smiled back. Because he had guessed what Henry was going to do.

"Say cheese, Squirt!" Henry said, and hurled the vacuum bag filled with cheese-puff powder over the heads of the slugs.

At the same time, Keats tossed the second-place pin like a dart. The pin hit the vacuum bag dead-on. It burst with a *pop!*, and the cheese-puff powder inside exploded all over the slugs.

For a moment everything in the alley went completely still. Then with a tiny *slurrrp,* one slug stuck out its tongue and licked the skin of a nearby slug.

Its eyes lit up.

Kablam! The slugs burst into motion. They started tasting and then nibbling on each other.

"Splurp! Splarb! Splarb!" Squirt shouted. But the slugs didn't listen. Their eyes went blank. They turned their teeth on each other, hungry for more cheese puffs.

Slugs gobbled up other slugs like piranhas in the Amazon. Squirt shrugged. He stopped *splarb*ing and joined in the feeding frenzy.

Keats couldn't watch anymore. He shut his eyes.

A minute later, the alley went very quiet. Keats opened his eyes. Henry was grinning at him. "How'd you like that World's Greatest Plan?" he asked.

Keats looked down.

"Whoa," he said. Just one slug remained. It was Squirt. Flopped on his back, he was too fat to turn over.

Henry crouched next to him. "Wow, that's amazing," he said.

"I know," Keats agreed. "Squirt ate all the other slugs!"

"No," Henry said, his grin getting bigger. "It's amazing because that's just what *you* look like after Thanksgiving dinner."

Keats rolled his eyes. "Ha, ha," he said. But then he laughed for real. "We did it!"

"We saved the town!" Henry clapped Keats on the back. "And we'll still make it back to the picnic in time for the fireworks!"

The cousins found a clear plastic box with

a lid in a nearby Dumpster. They picked up Squirt. He was as slimy as always but much easier to handle now that he was so full. Into the box he went.

As Henry and Keats shut the lid with a *click*, a long black limousine rolled into the alley. No one was driving, and the front seat was empty.

The back window of the limo rolled down. Mr. Cigam's cheery, diamond-shaped face popped into view. The elderly magician waved to the boys. He had a corn chip in his hand.

"Greetings, Henry and Keats!" he said.

"Hi, Mr. Cigam," Henry and Keats replied. They carried the box with Squirt over to the limo and set it down by a tire.

"Well done!" Mr. Cigam said. "You two must be hungry after such hard work. Snack?" He held a tray of chips up to the window. In

the center of the tray sat an open jar of nacho cheese dip.

Henry groaned. But Keats laughed. Mr. Cigam seemed clueless that they could have used the dip . . . a half hour ago.

"No thanks, Mr. Cigam," Keats said. "And I think you might lose your appetite after you see the store."

"Pish," Mr. Cigam said. "My magic is still good for something. I'll have the Purple Rabbit shipshape by morning."

"It's *your* store?" Henry asked.

Mr. Cigam nodded. "I used to visit daily. But lately, I've been feeling a bit . . . I don't know . . ."

"Turned around?" Keats guessed.

"Precisely." Mr. Cigam's smile dimmed. "In the old days, I'd never have feared a Wallenda slug. Even if that one slug *can* become a swarm after eating cheese puffs."

Henry waggled a finger at the magician. "Don't beat yourself up, Mr. Cigam. Those slugs are slime-time scary."

Mr. Cigam chuckled. "Too true," he said. "Now there's the matter of payment. Here you are." The chip in his hand changed suddenly into a gleaming gold coin. Henry's eyes went wide.

Keats hesitated. "Seriously, Mr. Cigam, the supermarket *is* a disaster zone."

"Kind of like you, cuz," Henry said. He scraped an orange glob of octopus off Keats's cheek. "I think we might have earned it."

Keats took a whiff and had to agree. He accepted the coin. "Thanks, Mr. Cigam!"

"Excellent," the magician said. "By the by, I have two stepsisters who could use your services. They might be in touch."

"You hear that, Keats?" Henry said. "We're getting to be real pros at magic! I can just hear everyone talking about us now. They'll all say—"

BURRRP!

The loud noise came from the box at their feet.

"Oh, right," Keats said. "We haven't introduced you."

"Mr. Cigam, this is one very stuffed slug named Squirt," Henry said. "Squirt, say hello to the nice magician."

As Mr. Cigam peered down at him, Squirt burped again. The slug stretched his plump body to form letters on the plastic box.

Henry crouched down next to him. "Keats, check this out," he said, grinning.

Keats stooped so he could read the letters, too. And then he laughed as Squirt wrote, **wats fer desrt?**

ABOUT THE AUTHOR

BILL DOYLE grew up in Michigan and wrote his first story—a funny whodunit—when he was eight. Since then, he's written other action-packed books for kids, like the Scream Team series, the Crime Through Time series, and the Behind Enemy Lines series. He lives in New York City with two sluggish, snack-loving dachshunds.

You can visit him online at billdoyle.net.